Sh...

Written by Jo Windsor

Illustrated by Brent Putze

Rigby

Shar is a puppy.

She ate the shoes.
"No, Shar!" said Mom.
"Not the shoes!"

3

She ate the book.
"No, Shar!" said Mom.
"Not the book!"

She ate the socks.
"No, Shar!" said Mom.
"Not the socks!"

She ate the slippers.
"Oh no!" said Mom.
"Look at my slippers!"

Shar ate the pillow.

"Go out!" said Mom.

"Out, out, out!"

Shar ate the cat's dinner.

She ate the cat's dish!

"Meowww!"
went the cat.

"Come here, Shar!"
said Mom.
"You poor, poor puppy!"

A Rebus Chart

She ate the  .

She ate the  .

She ate the  .

She ate the  .

She ate the  .

She ate the cat's .

 She ate the cat's 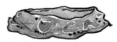 .

▬▬ Guide Notes

Title: Shar

Stage: Early (1) – Red

Genre: Fiction

Approach: Guided Reading

Processes: Thinking Critically, Exploring Language, Processing Information

Written and Visual Focus: Rebus writing

THINKING CRITICALLY
(sample questions)
* What do you think this story could be about?
* What do you know about puppies?
* How can you tell Shar is a puppy?
* Why do you think puppies like to eat things like books, socks, and shoes?
* How do you think Mom feels about Shar eating things?
* Look at page 9. What do you think will happen to Shar now?
* If Shar was your puppy, what would you do?
* Look at page 11. If you were the cat, what would you do?
* Look at page 14. How do you think Mom feels about Shar?

EXPLORING LANGUAGE

Terminology
Title, cover, illustrations, author, illustrator

Vocabulary
Interest words: slippers, pillow, poor
High-frequency words: is, just, a, she, no, said, the, look, at, they, out, you, go, went, come, here, are, not, my

Print Conventions
Capital letter for sentence beginnings and names (**Shar**, **M**om), periods, exclamation marks, quotation marks, commas